The Ins[illegible] Mary Girard

A Drama in One Act

by Lanie Robertson

A SAMUEL FRENCH ACTING EDITION

New York Hollywood London Toronto

SAMUELFRENCH.COM

ISBN 978-0-573-62227-4 Printed in U.S.A. #1165

For
ROSEMARY SEMINARA
whose support
and affection
has helped me
preserve
my own sanity.

THE INSANITY OF MARY GIRARD was first produced at The Painted Bride Art Center by Theatre Center Philadelphia on July 4, 1976. The producer was Albert Benzwie. It was directed by Cat Hebert; set and lighting designs by Cat Hebert; the production stage manager was Boris Grant. The cast, in order of appearance, was as follows:

MARY GIRARD .... Aldonna Page*

THE WARDER .... Parry Kraatz

MRS. LUM .... Sandy Rose

STEPHEN GIRARD .... Cat Hebert

MR. PHILIPS .... Christopher Whalen

POLLY KENTON .... Bonnilu Young

MRS. HATCHER .... Rebecca Goldstein

* Ms. Page was later replaced by Donna Dundon.

CHARACTER DESCRIPTIONS

MARY GIRARD: Mary is 29 years old, very pretty, strong peasant woman. Her coloring is dark, her hair long. She wears a fashionable, expensive dress.

THE WARDER: A strong man, Mary's age or older. He is dressed in knee breeches and barefoot. He wears a puff-sleeved shirt that is open at the neck and the sleeves are rolled up.

MRS. LUM: Mary's mother is in her late 40's. She wears good, clean clothes, but nothing fancy. She has a small lace skull cap on her head, a plain dress, and a shawl.

STEPHEN GIRARD: Mr. Girard is 39 years old. He is immaculately dressed in a fancy suit of frock coat and knee breeches, white socks and fine leather shoes, possibly of patent leather.

MR. PHILLIPS: Is the same age as Mr. Girard, and his appearance is very similar to that of Mr. Girard except that his clothing is all much rougher of texture. He should give the impression that "there but for the grace of God" goes Mr. Girard.

POLLY KENTON: Polly is about the same age as Mary. She is very pretty and does not have the rough strength of Mary. She appears both more intelligent and more sophisticated than Mary. She wears a lace cap, a fine but plain dress of expensive material. A gold watch is pinned to her bosom.

MRS. HATCHER: A woman in middle age. She is poor and dresses very plainly, with matching white cap and apron. Her dress is simple and of cheap material.

CHARACTERS
(In Order of Their Appearance)

MARY GIRARD, a very attractive woman of 29 years.

THE FURIES, three women, two men of any age.

THE WARDER, a man of middle age.

MRS. LUM, Mary's mother.

STEPHEN GIRARD, Mary's husband, ten years her senior.

MR. PHILLIPS, a steward of Pennsylvania Hospital and a man in his forties.

POLLY KENTON, a young woman.

MRS. HATCHER, a woman approximately Mary's own age.

TIME: A Saturday night in the Fall of 1790.

PLACE: A lunatic cell in the basement of the Pennsylvania Hospital in Philadelphia.

NOTE: Although the events presented in this play are based on fact, there has been no attempt to accurately portray the personalities of those responsible for the incarceration of Mrs. Stephen Girard.

CHORUS: The FURIES should be presented in the following way:

FURY #1 should play the role of THE WARDER.

FURY #2 should play the role of MRS. LUM.

FURY #3 should play the role of POLLY KENTON.

FURY #4 should play the role of MR. PHILLIPS.

FURY #5 should play the role of MRS. HATCHER.

Fury #1 should think of himself as a "regressed child."

Fury #2 should have "delusions of grandeur."

Fury #3 should be an "obsessive/compulsive."

Fury #4 should be "active/passive" usually in a catatonic state.

Fury #5 should be an "hysteric."

The segments of lines should be almost equally divided among Furies 1, 2, 3, and 5. Fury #4 should say much less but always the "Dr. Rush" references. Fury #5 should deliver most of the "God" and "Jesus" words, etc.

The Insanity of Mary Girard

AT RISE *the stage is bare except for* MARY GIRARD *who is seated, bound in the* TRANQUILIZING CHAIR. *This is a device used for "excitable patients" who were insane or believed to be. There are leather straps to bind down the wrists, the arms, the chest and thighs, iron rings to go about the ankles, and a square box that swings down over the head. As the* LIGHTS *gradually* COME UP, *several figures* ENTER *from different directions. These are the* FURIES. *They circle about the chair. One of them lifts the box and we see* MARY's *face for the first time.*

MARY GIRARD *is a very attractive woman, twenty-nine years old. Her eyes and hair are dark. She seems at first asleep or in a coma. Then she becomes very aggitated and strains against her bonds.*

FURIES. (*Tauntingly.*) Mary. Mary Girard. Polly. Polly. Polly-Mary. Girard.

MARY. (*Screams.*) Who are you? Stay away from me. No. Let me out of here. Do you hear me? Set me free at once.

FURIES. Oh, she wants. To be set. Free. At once. Oh, no. We mustn't. Do that.

MARY. Set me free, I tell you. Who are you? How dare you laugh at me! How dare you!

FURIES. Oh. She's so. Indig. Nant. Quite the fine lady. Isn't she? No one would think. Her husband was. Well-to-do. Would they, Mary?

MARY. What do you want of me? Did you come here to torment me?

FURIES. We want nothing, Mary. Only to comfort you. To aid you. Be with you in time of travail. Do whatever we can. Or may. Or might.

MARY. Then for God's sake set me free. If I stay in this chair any longer I shall go mad.

FURIES. Oh, say that and. We'll never let you out. Dr. Rush's chair is always successful. Such a good doctor! Dr. Rush!

MARY. Please set me free. Please!

FURIES. Does she promise? To behave? Would she try? To run? Away?

MARY. No. I promise I won't run away. I won't.

FURIES. Besides. She has no place. To run. Except into the wall.Which we can do, but not her. Not you, Mary. Not you.

MARY. Who are you? What are you? Tell me.

FURIES. We're no one. Nothing. Inmates of the asylum. Like you, Mary. Figments of your imagination. Air. Less than. Smoke. A puff. A poof. Of nothing. Nothing, nothing. Nothing. (*The* FURIES *set* MARY *free.*)

MARY. If you are nothing, then I must be mad. I can see you, hear you. (MARY *grabs at them but they elude her.*)

FURIES. No, you mustn't touch us. For then we would have to. Tear you apart. We don't exist. We are ghosts. Your friends. Selves of yourself. Fiends and angels. We know nothing. Except everything. You know. Or want. To know.

MARY. You know everything I want to know?

FURIES. Certainly. Assuredly. Definitely.

MARY. Then tell me. Tell me everything I want to know.

FURIES. What do you? Want to know, Mary?

MARY. Tell me where I am? And how long I've been here.

FURIES. (*Disappointed.*) That's too simple. It's no fun. You know that already. The Penn. Sylvania. Hospital. The same. As it was. This morning.

MARY. This morning? How long have I been here?

FURIES. It's the same day. As it was before.

MARY. I can't have been here only a matter of hours. It's not possible! Oh, being in that chair is horrible. Horrible!

FURIES. Of course, it's horrible. It's supposed. To be. That's what you. Get for. Being crazy. Crazy Mary Girard.

MARY. But I'm not crazy. You know I'm not.

FURIES. You must be! Mr. Girard had you admitted. As a lunatic, paying patient. The doctors have agreed. To keep you here. As long as Mr. Girard. Continues to pay. Your bills. And quite a lucrative account. You'll prove to be. For a lunatic, Mary.

MARY. (FURIES *laugh at her frustration thru this.*) It's all a misunderstanding. When I see the doctors, when I speak to Mr. Girard, it will all be corrected. It's a mistake, I tell you. And that chair. I thought I'd go mad.

FURIES. She will. In time. She sounds positively. Stark raving. Mad. That chair is one of the. Prized possessions. And inventions of. Dr. Rush. He positively. Loves it. And. So do we.

MARY. I couldn't move. I couldn't see anything. No sooner was I strapped into it than I began to itch.

FURIES. Nerves. Only nerves. Or madness.

MARY. I couldn't even scratch my arm. And then my eyes began to tear and I couldn't wipe them. And there was such a roaring in my ears. I thought I would go . . . that it would drive me. . . .

FURIES. Yes? Go. On. Don't stop. We want. To hear. Everything.

MARY. All sounds were strange, distant, as though I were under water, drowned without being dead, and it seemed so terribly hard to breath. Later I fell asleep and had such dreams that I woke up screaming. Then I thought I was being smothered, coldly, carefully smothered with an enormous pillow that kept getting larger and larger. First it seemed the size of that box, but then it was as large as the room. Then it grew to the size of the entire hospital. And I knew that it would continue growing. Smothering not only me but everyone. The size of the city. And then the state. And then the size of the entire United States. And I awoke screaming.

FURIES. And you see. No one was. Smothering you at all. You were only here. Experiencing the effects. Of the Tranquilizing Chair.

MARY. And the echo in the box of my own screams . . . It was horrible! Oh why would they put me in such a thing? Surely they know I'm not mad.

FURIES. But it's the. Proper treatment. For your type. Of madness. Everybody knows. There are two kinds of. Madness. The Torpid. And those subject to. Excitation. Dr. Rush. Has invented. Two appliances. To be used for. The treatment of. The mad. The gyrator. Or revolving machine. That shakes them up. The other is. The tranquilizing chair. For types like you. Ones subject to. Excitation. Or claims of. Sanity.

MARY. I feel weak, faint.

FURIES. It's only natural. After the. Bloodletting.

MARY. Bloodletting?

FURIES. It's quite regular. Quite customary. Mary.

Quite natural. It lessens greatly. Your protestations. Of sanity. From you they took. Thirty ounces. Of blood.

MARY. Was that the itching of my arm?

FURIES. Yes, you see. You didn't feel. A thing. You see how well. The chair works. Now, Mary?

MARY. Ah! I must get out of here. I must. I can't have been here for only one day. It isn't possible.

FURIES. Less. It's only now. Near midnight. Soon it will be Sunday. You'll be able to hear. The bells. From all the churches. Stephen Girard will be in his usual pew. Mary. Praying for your soul. No doubt.

MARY. (FURIES *laugh throughout.*) I must see him, talk with him. I'll ask him to forgive me or to let me pass away to some other place, pass out of his life as though we'd never met.

FURIES. The idea! Did you ever? Hear of such a thing? Horrid. Shocking. Disgraceful. A dreadful idea. For a married woman. To have. Leave her husband? She must be. Mad.

MARY. If you know anything about me you know that my marriage was the worst thing that ever happened to me. Until this.

FURIES. The hussy! I must say. I'm shocked. And this from. A woman legally bound. To a husband for thirteen years. She sounds like. A woman of. The streets. A common whore. A bawdy house tart. A ten-penny slut.

MARY. (*Furious.*) How dare you speak to me like that. I'm Mrs. Stephen Girard! I don't have to tolerate your taunts and jeers. Get out. Get away from me and get out!

FURIES. (*Afraid of being sent out.*) Oh, No, don't, Mary. Don't send us off. Or shut us out. We're only trying. To help you. Mary. To put mildly. What you're bound to hear. Tomorrow. Only then it will be. So very much. Worse.

MARY. No one would dare talk to me in such a manner!

FURIES. They will, Mary. And worse. Much worse, Mary. The ones on the streets. The ones at those windows. The ones who come daily. To stare and point. And laugh at the lunatics. To mock them. Try to frighten them into fits. Or convulsions. Or seizures. Of the most horrid kinds. And it works beautifully, Mary. You'll be surprised how often. And how violently the seizures come.

MARY. I don't believe you. I don't believe there are people like that, people who do things like that. It's . . . cruel. People aren't like that. I'm sure they're not.

FURIES. (*Laughing.*) She has so much. To learn. You mustn't undervalue the power of an accusing finger. The amusement people derive from the suffering of others. The superiority they feel when they see those less fortunate. They relish it. Revel in it. Rejoice for it.

MARY. It mustn't be allowed. I'll speak to someone about it.

FURIES. (*In glee.*) Speak to someone! Mustn't be allowed! Glorious! Wonderful. Mary, can't you see how large? The windows were made? So the people wouldn't have to stoop? To see in?

MARY. They'll not look at me. Not here. I couldn't stand it. I'll be gone before they come. And if I'm not I'll hide from them. Under the covers of the bed or under the bed if necessary. I won't have them laughing at me. I couldn't stand it, I tell you.

FURIES. No! Poor Mary. If you hide. It'll make matters. So much worse. The attendants will pull you out. Chain you there where the manacles are. Facing the windows. No, Mary. It's much better. If you don't hide.

MARY. You said you know all I want to know. Then tell me how to get out of here. Please. Please.

FURIES. We can only. Show you. Yes, show you. You have to start. At the beginning. By seeing. The warder of. The cells.

MARY. But I saw him this morning. He won't help me.

FURIES. You have to. See him for. He's the beginning. And if you are to. Know the end. You have to begin at the. Start. (FURIES *place a short cape on* MARY's *shoulders, a muff on her hands, and a hat on her head.* WARDER *enters. He is a young man about* MARY's *age.*)

WARDER. Here ye go. This way. In here, Mary. That's yer name, ain't it?

MARY. My name is Mrs. Stephen Girard. You will call me by that name if you address me again.

WARDER. Oh no, I don't. I calls ye Mary. I have it on strictest orders not to call ye any such false name as that.

MARY. I am Mrs. Girard. There is nothing false about that.

WARDER. Oh, well, ye'll be right at home. We got the Queen of France an' the King of Poland in here, too. Call yerself whatever ye will. It'll cut no ice with me. I calls ye Mary because I was told by Mr. Girard hisself I was to so call ye.

MARY. But you know who I am. You came to my home in your carriage to bring me to see the doctor. You know I'm Mrs. Girard.

WARDER. I went to Mr. Girard's home. Not yers.

All I know is yer Mary. More than that I don't want to know.

MARY. But I'm his wife, Mary Girard.

WARDER. I'm tellin' ye true. It's Mary ye be and Mary ye'll remain as far as I'm concerned. Unless ye take to bein' the Queen of Sheba or somebody else. Then I'll be callin' ye that.

MARY. (*Handing him some money.*) Look, I have some money. . . .

WARDER. (*Taking it.*) Oh, ye'll be glad ye give this to me. I'll see ye get some real food some of the time. Somethin' to keep up yer strength instead of this gruel all the time. Maybe a pint a somethin' warmin' on occasion, huh?

MARY. You don't understand. I came to see the doctor, and you're to take me back to my home at once.

WARDER. Home? This room's yer home now, Mary. It's cheery, too, in daylight. That is, if ye'll be able to see much daylight fer all the admirers ye'll be entertainin' in them winders up there.

MARY. What admirers?

WARDER. Tomorrow's sabbath. Lots of folks'll be out an' in a holiday mood. You'll see fer yerself then, I figure.

MARY. I won't be here tomorrow. I came to see the doctor about a . . . a personal condition. Where is he, sir?

WARDER. Me name's Frankie. Ye be good to Frankie, an' Frankie'll be good to ye, too, Mary. (*Pause.*)

MARY. I demand that you take me to the doctor at once.

WARDER. Snooty, ain't ye. Wants to see the doctor at once, do she? Well, doctors don't come round at once. They're due sometime week after next. I guess ye'll wait till then, all right. I'll just take yer hat an' cape an' muff so's ye can get to feelin' right at home, Mary.

MARY. Stay away from me!

WARDER. If that's the way ye want it. (*Calls.*) Aides here! (FURIES *enter and snatch* MARY'S *cape, muff and hat from her.*)

MARY. No, stop. Please. You mustn't do this. (FURIES *exit.*)

WARDER. Oh, things will be worst by a yard if ye act like that too frequent.

MARY. Do you have any idea who my husband is?

WARDER. Yep. I know who ye claims he be.

MARY. He's the wealthiest man in the city of Philadelphia.

WARDER. Wouldn't serprize me a notch.

MARY. Possibly the wealthiest in all the Republic.

WARDER. Yep. That too. (*Pause.*)

MARY. (*Speaking rapidly.*) If you keep me here against my will, you will be making a terrible mistake. He might sue this hospital, its board of directors, you and everyone connected with it.

WARDER. Nope. Don't think so. Seems I know more 'bout yer Mr. Girard than ye do, Mary.

MARY. I doubt that anyone in your position would know anything at all about the likes of Mr. Girard. But your superiors will.

WARDER. All I know is that it was Mr. Girard hisself who said yer lunatick an' asked most kindly that ye be put here. That's all I know.

MARY. That's a lie. How dare you impugn my husband's name with such a lie.

WARDER. Some says ye done some of that impugnin' yerself, Mary Girard.

MARY. (*Striking at him.*) How dare you! (WARDER *ducks her blow and slips out of the cell. He closes the door.*)

MARY. What are you doing?

WARDER. Lockin' the door to yer new home. It's customary.

MARY. You can't keep me here. You cannot. Where am I? Is this a prison? What authority do you have to do this? I want to go home. Please. Don't do this to me! Please! Please!

WARDER. I'm only doin' what I gets paid for doin'. It's my job. I only takes orders from 'em what's higher up, Mary.

MARY. But surely you can see this is wrong.

WARDER. There yer wrong, Mary. I'm not paid to see what's right or wrong. It's not my business. My business is lockin' ye up. The rest is not my business.

(*The* FURIES *enter laughing.*)

MARY. You will drive me mad.

WARDER. It's not my business. My business is lockin' ye up. The rest is not my business.

MARY. You will drive me mad!

WARDER. It's not my business. My business is lockin' ye up. The rest is not my business.

MARY. Answer me! Is this a prison?

WARDER. That's real insultin', that is. This is the Pennsylvania Hospital. Founded by Mr. Franklin hisself, for treatment of sick poor folk. Lucky fer him he died this year, otherwise he might be highly offended by the way yer talkin' 'bout his fine hospital. An' ye are in the ward fer the mentally deranged. The place fer lunaticks, in plain speech.

MARY. But I'm not a lunatic.

WARDER. That's not fer ye or me to say. That's fer Mr. Girard to say. He be yer legal guardian an' he's the one who put ye here.

MARY. Stop saying that. I won't permit you to lie about him that way. He . . . he would never do . . . do anything . . . I don't believe you . . . but even if he did, he hasn't the authority. He's no doctor. He's not medically qualified to pronounce me either sane or insane.

WARDER. He's yer husband, ain't he? This Stephen Girard?

MARY. Yes.

WARDER. Well then, thar ye be. He don't got to be no doctor. All he gotta be is yer husband. That makes him yer legal guardian an' by law whenever a legal guardian says the one they's guardian over is lunatick then we picks 'em up and puts 'em here. We got lots of women folks here whose helpmates has writ out a little letter sayin' they's lunatick. You'll see 'em. They's crazy, too. Seems to happen more to women folks 'count of the delicacy of thar minds.

MARY. Look at me, sir. You can tell I am not . . . like those others.

WARDER. Oh, lots of crazy folks looks jus' fine when they come in here. I jus' give you 'bout a month. I bet I won't be able to tell you from any of those others. Wait an' see if I can.

MARY. For God's sake, sir, look at me. Do I appear to be without my reason?

WARDER. Have ye not heard the wive's tale, niver judge a book by its cover?

MARY. But I tell you I'm sane.

WARDER. Yep. That's what most of 'em thinks, too.

MARY. Listen to me. Even though Mr. Girard is my legal guardian, surely someone, someone must make out some legal document declaring me insane. Isn't that true?

WARDER. Right as rain.

MARY. Well, this has to be a dreadful mistake because no one has examined me. My husband said I was to come with you to see a doctor.

WARDER. Yep. That's what we tell most of 'em. "Jest goin' to the hospital to see the doctor." Works nearly every time. Sometimes tell 'em they're goin' to see the dentist. Jest for variety's sake. An' I got the legal an' bindin' written document from Mr. Shepherd, hisself, one of the managers of the whole hospital. He's got a little letter from Mr. Girard sayin' straight out that ye, his wife, Mary Girard, is lunatick an' requestin' that ye be held here fer treatment fer the rest of yer natural life. Lest a course ye be cured.

MARY. For God's sake don't jest with me, sir.

WARDER. Oh, no, it's no jest. (*He locks the lock.*) Ye can be sure the locks here are the finest and the realest locks ye'll ever see. Also, yer companions. They're the genuine thing. Out an' out lunyticks, ever last one. I'll jest get the good Dr. Rush's tranquilizin' chair fer ye. I think yer sorta subject to excitations. Ye'll feel better then. See if ye don't. (*He exits.*)

(*The* FURIES *enter.*)

FURIES. Don't be. Upset. Mary. Mary. That one's past. You can forget. All about that one, Mary.

MARY. I have to get out of here. I have to see someone, talk with someone. When will they let me see someone?

FURIES. But we can let you. See anyone. You choose. Just tell us who it is. Name the name. And instantly you'll see them.

MARY. Will you truly or am I only imagining this?

FURIES. What does it. Matter, Mary? Give us the names.

MARY. I want to see my mother.

FURIES. Her mother! Oh, how funny! Little Mary wants to see her mother!

MARY. Yes. Let me see her. Please. (FURIES *exit.* MRS. LUM *enters.*)

MRS. LUM. Madam, you sent for me?

MARY. Mother? Mother, you've come to me?

MRS. LUM. Rise, madam. Of course I would come at the bidding of Mrs. Girard. I could hardly do otherwise, could I? Although I cannot pretend to understand why you wanted me here.

MARY. Oh, I need you, mother.

MRS. LUM. Need me, madam? You never needed me very much, and now I'm sure you need me not at all. You mustn't speak extravagantly. Surely there is nothing I can do for you that you haven't the wherewithall to do much better than I.

MARY. It isn't money that I need from you.

MRS. LUM. I should think not.

MARY. It is comfort that I need of you, now.

MRS. LUM. Comfort? You live in the very heart of comfort, madam. Never have I seen a house this fine, furnishings this rich. The shine on these floors makes me afraid to take a step, lest they prove to be glass and crack underfoot. Everything here shines like lights from a great tower. You must be quite happy here.

MARY. What are you saying? This is not my house. This is a cell for lunatics in the cellar of the great hospital. Do not mock me, madam. Surely you see it is cold and damp and horrid here.

MRS. LUM. I see only that when you married above your station it brought you great rewards. I see also why you did not want your family coming here, trapsing the dirt from workmen's feet across the polish of your fine wood floors.

MARY. My family was not welcome here. Neither were my friends. And now I myself am not. I told you whenever I visited you what things were like for me. You must have believed me, didn't you?

MRS. LUM. A poor excuse beats none, they say.

MARY. You didn't believe me. You never did, did you! You thought I didn't want you here because I was ashamed of you.

MRS. LUM. Something like that, yes. It's all right. We understood. We knew that it would heppen. Happens all the time. It's all right. It's to be expected.

MARY. But it wasn't me at all. It was Mr. Girard. He didn't want you here.

MRS. LUM. That's all right too. Why should he? We wasn't kin to him, and I won't listen to you berate Mr. Girard. He was a prince to your father. An absolute prince. Kept him working on his ships as long as your father was alive. I'll not listen to any bad words about Mr. Girard.

MARY. Mother, my husband abuses me.

MRS. LUM. For shame that you should give him cause. And double shame that you be brazen enough to tell it. You should have learned by now that there is nothing unusual in a husband's abusing his wife. It is the woman's place to be clever enough to seem to do his will whether she do or no. If you have been married this longish time, Madam, and still not learned that, I do not doubt that you have made a sorry time for yourself and for poor Mr. Girard as well.

MARY. And must the wife always bend to her husband's will, whether it be right or wrong?

MRS. LUM. Most assuredly, for it is the husband's place to rule his wife. The woman's to obey her husband.

MARY. And why must it be so?

MRS. LUM. Because it is the Law.

MARY. Whose Law?

MRS. LUM. God's Law. When you married you vowed to honor and obey your husband, madam, 'till death do you part. Do you dare question the Law of God Himself?

MARY. If it is unjust. . . .

MRS. LUM. It is not possible for God's Law to be unjust.

MARY. If this is God's Law, as you say it is, why didn't you explain this Law to me before I married Mr. Girard?

MRS. LUM. You were a woman, madam.

MARY. I was sixteen years old. I was a girl.

MRS. LUM. It was your wish to marry.

MARY. It was Mr. Girard's wish to marry me.

MRS. LUM. You were not so innocent as that, madam. Your marriage was a financial transaction. Your father and I . . . You knew that Mr. Girard had money and that you would never have to work another day in your life if you married him.

MARY. Then why did you speak to me about love and home?

MRS. LUM. Because I knew it would be easier for you if you loved him.

MARY. But you know I didn't. I was a servant. I wanted a home of my own.

MRS. LUM. You knew what you were doing. You got the home you wanted and much more. The shine of this house blinds the eye.

MARY. Look about you. Nothing you see here is mine. I have nothing, Madam, nothing.

MRS. LUM. Then you can only blame yourself. A wise woman never lets her husband know the distaste she may feel for him. You should have dissembled more and hidden whatever loathing you may have felt behind a display of feigned affection.

MARY. I would have been a liar.

MRS. LUM. You would have fared better. (*Pause.*)

MARY. I asked you here because I have desperate news. (*Pause.*) I am with child.

MRS. LUM. Polly! This is wonderful!

MARY. No. . . .

MRS. LUM. Nothing in all the world can do more to please a childless man. Mr. Girard must be overjoyed.

MARY. No.

MRS. LUM. You mean he is not?

MARY. I haven't told him.

MRS. LUM. But you must, at once.

MARY. I cannot.

MRS. LUM. What do you mean you cannot?

MARY. I fear for my safety, mother. I fear what he might do to me.

MRS. LUM. Do to you?

MARY. It is not Mr. Girard's child.

MRS. LUM. Polly! No!

MARY. I have informed Mr. Girard that I intend to leave his house. I want to come home again. I can bring you nothing but my gratitude and a still fond regard for you.

MRS. LUM. I cannot help you, madam. It would have been well for you to have had his child.

MARY. Don't you think I tried to have a child by him?

MRS. LUM. All I know is that you have stupidly jeopardized not only your own welfare but . . . but everything else . . . as well. If Mr. Girard repudiates you, so must I. If Mr. Girard repudiates you, so must I.

MARY. No! Don't leave me! Don't leave! (*To*

FURIES.) She didn't even see me here. She thought that I was still mistress of my house. But I wasn't.

FURIES. You never. Were. Were you, Mary?

MARY. What? Leave me alone. You cheated me. I want to see my mother here.

FURIES. Do you think? Do you imagine? Do you suppose? That it would make. The slightest bit. Of difference?

MARY. Yes. Yes, it would. I know it. When she sees me here, sees what they have done to me.

FURIES. But she. Won't! Mary. She won't. Why should. She? She'll get. From Mr. Girard. The little help. She's always. Wanted. She'll not come. Here. Again.

MARY. You're lying to me. Lying!

FURIES. We? You're doing it. To yourself. We want you to see. How things are. With you. How things are. Are. Are. With you.

(*Lights up on* MR. PHILLIPS *and* STEPHEN GIRARD.)

MR. GIRARD. "How things are with her." What do you mean by that?

MR. PHILLIPS. Dr. Rush asked that I speak to you personally, Mr. Girard, to make known to you certain surprising developments that have only now come to our attention regarding the state or condition of your wife, sir.

MR. GIRARD. I do not know, sir, if you value your time, but I do mine. Please be brief.

MR. PHILLIPS. I will try. May I sit, sir?

MR. GIRARD. By all means, sit or do whatever you wish, only let us get this bothersome business settled. If there is some question as to the adequacy of the monthly payment of her expenses I shall naturally increase the allotment to whatever sum is necessary, although I will remind you that both you and Dr. Hutchinson assured me the amount settled on was more than sufficient.

MR. PHILLIPS. Oh, no, Mr. Girard. Let me assure you that it is not a question of costs. The generosity of your settlement is well-known by all concerned in this matter. No, the hospital could not wish for a more beneficial arrangement. No sir, it is not a financial matter that brings me here but rather one concerning your wife's mental and . . . physical condition.

MR. GIRARD. As I am quite familiar with the one and not at all interested in the other, I doubt that anything you have to tell me could be of the least interest to me. Nonetheless, as she yet remains my wife, and as you have taken it upon yourself to interrupt my affairs with this matter, I am willing to listen to you, only briefly.

MR. PHILLIPS. I have rather surprising news for you and for all of us at the hospital. Mrs. Girard is with child.

MR. GIRARD. Yes.

MR. PHILLIPS. Do you mean, sir, you have been cognizant of that fact?

MR. GIRARD. I have.

MR. PHILLIPS. And were you so aware when you had her brought to us?

MR. GIRARD. Yes, sir, I was.

MR. PHILLIPS. And yet you brought her to us to be confined with the mentally insane?

MR. GIRARD. Most certainly. I find it curious that I need point out to you that physical conditions have nothing whatsoever to do with the state of one's mind. I brought my wife to you because she is insane. That has nothing to do with whatever physical condition she may be in.

MR. PHILLIPS. Mr. Girard, I am happy to tell you that is not always the case. Although it is true that the mind functions separately from the body which supports it, there is one major exception to that general rule.

MR. GIRARD. And what is that?

MR. PHILLIPS. The state of pregnancy. It is not uncommon for a woman with child to exhibit many of the signs we ordinarilly ascribe only to the insane. You see, many of the irregularities you spoke of are quite possibly due to nothing more than the naturally flighty state of mind brought on in many women by the physical changes in the female body during the pre-natal period. When a woman is with child she is wont to have imaginings, to suffer strange cravings, certain outbursts of temper and language that one does not expect. In other words, her behavior may become erratic in a fashion that is often alarming to those who are used to a more sedate and stately behavior on the part of the lady. Consequently, under these circumstances, the board of directors and I agree that it is in everyone's best interest for you to remove Mrs. Girard from our care, allow her the confinement usually recommended for the later stages of a pregnancy, and, after her deliverance of your child, she will most probably prove to be as sane as she ever was. What I am trying to tell you, sir, is the happy news that Mrs. Girard is quite possibly, even probably, as sane as you or I. (*Pause.*)

MR. GIRARD. My wife, sir, is insane.

MR. PHILLIPS. Mr. Girard . . .

MR. GIRARD. (*Interrupting.*) I said, she is insane. (*Slight pause.*)

MR. PHILLIPS. Your wife suffers from severe headaches. She is extremely nervous. Upon occasion she has exhibited erratic behavior, and outbursts of abusive language. If she were not pregnant, there might be cause to think an extended rest, close care, and quiet might not be enough to restore her normal faculties. However, as she *is* with child . . .

MR. GIRARD. That is a fact I wish you and the members of the board to disregard. Whether she is, as you say, with child or not need be no concern of yours. Nor of anyone else's. I tell you in all candor it is not a fact I wish ever to be known. Nor do I feel kindly disposed toward you, sir, for your having pressed this loathsome fact to my consideration. True, I was previously aware of . . . her condition. But I have chosen of my own free will to ignore it. It is my wish, sir, that you and all the members of the board do likewise.

MR. PHILLIPS. Sir, I am amazed. I have just told you that your wife is soon to be delivered of your child, a child you seem determined will be gestated and born in a madhouse, amidst scenes of the most horrid chaos, amongst madmen and madwomen, and you advise me to ignore it?

MR. GIRARD. Precisely.

MR. PHILLIPS. Mr. Girard, I am trying to tell you that given these newly discovered circumstances we cannot permit you to leave Mrs. Girard in these conditions. Indeed, to place such a woman in such surroundings at such a time is to pose the greatest possible threat to her sanity, no matter how sound of mind she might have been beforehand.

MR. GIRARD. I see. (*He writes out a draft.*) Perhaps this will be sufficient. (*He hands the check out to* MR. PHILLIPS, *but* PHILLIPS *does not take it.*)

MR. PHILLIPS. Mr. Girard. It is not a question of money, sir.

MR. GIRARD. Is that fact?

MR. PHILLIPS. It is, sir.

MR. GIRARD. Come, come, sir. I am a loyal and an active supporter of our new republic, and I am a businessman. In both capacities it has been my experience that everything in life is a question of money. I have found no friendship, no love, no loyalty, and no fact that cannot be altered by a large enough draft or a tidy enough sum of money.

MR. PHILLIPS. Surely you can't believe that, Mr. Girard.

MR. GIRARD. Believe it? I know it. It is fact, sir. I have staked my career on it, and, as you can see, I have prospered. (MR. GIRARD *thrusting the check at him.*) Look at this!

MR. PHILLIPS. (*Taking the check.*) Three thousand dollars. But this is made out . . .

MR. GIRARD. To you, sir. That is payment in advance which I hope you will be gracious enough to accept from me. You see, I do not choose to be concerned any further with any difficulties that may arise due to my wife's . . . confinement. Therefore, I humbly ask that you personally see to it that whatever needs be done is done to keep all references to her, her child, if it should live, and any other difficulties concerning her, beyond my awareness. As to the board of trustees, tell them I will assume all responsibility for this matter, in writing, of course. Tell them, also, that within a month of my unfortunate wife's demise the hospital shall receive a check identical to the one you hold now. You need not ever mention this check. I feel a man's finances are no one's affair but his own. Tell them, also, that upon my death, I will bequeath

Pennsylvania Hospital no less a sum than ten times the amount written there. All this, of course, to be above and beyond the sums already agreed to for her daily care, and given in deepest gratitude for the superb treatment accorded the insane woman who unfortunately still bears my name.

MR. PHILLIPS. I don't know what to say.

MR. GIRARD. Answer only this: can it be done?

MR. PHILLIPS. Yes. (*Lights.*)

MR. GIRARD. Answer only this: can it be done?

MR. PHILLIPS. Yes.

MR. GIRARD. Good! See to it then. I believe you know your way out?

MR. PHILLIPS. But, sir . . .

MR. GIRARD. Sir?

MR. PHILLIPS. What of the child?

MR. GIRARD. That, sir, is no concern of mine.

MR. PHILLIPS. I would not have a child of mine born under such conditions for all the money in the world.

MR. GIRARD. And I can assure you, sir, neither would I.

MR. PHILLIPS. Mr. Girard. Do you mean the child . . .

MR. GIRARD. I bid you good day, sir.

MR. PHILLIPS. Sir. (*Lights fade on* GIRARD *and* PHILLIPS. FURIES *set* MARY *free.*)

MARY. No, Mr. Phillips, don't go. Please don't go.

FURIES. He can't. Hear you. Mary.

MARY. He can. I know he can. He looked right at me.

FURIES. He can't hear you. Because he doesn't. Want to. Men lose all their faculties. If the profit's sound.

MARY. Mr. Phillips!

FURIES. He can't hear you, Mary. He won't hear you. No. Body. Will. Poor Mary. Poor Mary Girard.

MARY. What will become of my child?

FURIES. Whose baby is it., Mary? Yes, tell us, Mary. Tell us who the father is. Tell us. Tell. Tell.

MARY. The father is unimportant. He was someone warm and affectionate to me.

FURIES. You were untrue, Mary. You cuckolded your husband. You betrayed him. And broke your marriage vows. For shame. Shame, Mary. You will give birth to an evil thing. Only evil comes from evil. Something dark and horrid comes from evil. Darkness bred in darkness gives forth darkness.

MARY. I don't believe it. I don't believe you. You're trying to drive me mad.

FURIES. You should have been like. Polly. Kenton. Yes, definitely. Like Polly. Then you would have. Been all right. Had your baby. And your home. Your mother would have. Been so. Grateful. Mrs. Lum would have. Loved. Having a. Daughter like. Polly.

MARY. What are you saying?

FURIES. Polly. Polly. Polly.

MARY. I am Polly.

FURIES. Polly. Polly Mary. Polly Mary Girard. Crazy Mary Girard. Yes, now. But not soon. No, not soon. Soon the whole city will know. Mr. Girard's Polly. They will have. Forgotten you. Mary. Even your mother. If she were alive. Would favor. Polly.

MARY. What are you talking about? (*The* FURIES *exit leaving* POLLY KENTON.)

POLLY. They were talking about me, Mrs. Girard.

MARY. Who are you? What are you doing here? I don't know you!

POLLY. My name's Polly, Polly Kenton. There's no reason why it should be important to you. I'm only one of a long line of housekeepers who'll replace you, Mrs. Girard.

MARY. You admit that to my face?

POLLY. I'm not important really. Only one in a long line of girls and women he will turn to, has turned to already. You know that.

MARY. Yes, I know it. I know that Sally Bickham, the slut. He brought her into my house. Called her his housekeeper. Tried to keep me out of town so I couldn't see she'd taken over my room. And you! You're just like her, is that it?

POLLY. In a way, just like her.

MARY. And there will be others, too, I suppose.

POLLY. I'm sure there will be.

MARY. And so you're a whore just like all the others.

(*Pause.*)

POLLY. I'm his housekeeper, Mrs. Girard. The difference is that I will be more successful and longer lasting than the rest. He will even come to care for me a little, as much as he is able to care for a woman, anyway.

MARY. I don't believe you.

POLLY. I wouldn't lie to you, Mrs. Girard, because I have no need to do so. (*Pause.*)

MARY. Why didn't he care for me?

POLLY. In the beginning he did. You should have had his child.

MARY. But it wasn't my fault we didn't have children. Oh, I thought it was. And I knew he blamed me. He didn't say anything, but sometimes as I was sewing I'd suddenly feel cold, as though a draft of icy wind had pierced me, and I'd look up and see him staring at me. Only that. Only staring. And I knew he was looking at me as though I were a column of figures that didn't quite balance in his cash books.

Later, he started taking me to doctors. They said that I was a "nervous woman". So he would send me into the country to cure my "nerves". Then I began to have these terrible headaches. And I hated to be around him, for I knew he felt I'd swindled him because I couldn't give him a son.

POLLY. You sound as though you wanted him to care for you.

MARY. Is that so strange?

POLLY. It isn't practical. You should have known what you could get from him and what you could not. You should have known what he expected in return and seen to it that you gave it to him.

MARY. His affection was all I wanted.

POLLY. But he had none to give. Wealth was what he had to give you.

MARY. That was nothing to me, nothing.

POLLY. If you had given him a baby you would have completed your side of the bargain. He, in turn, would have given you his undying gratitude. And if you could have managed to have a son, you would have won his affection as well.

MARY. But we could not have children. We tried and we could not.

POLLY. You should have seen to it that you had a child, even if it was not his. He would have thought it his, and the bargain would have been complete. You would have won his affection.

MARY. Must it be like a business tranaction?

POLLY. All relationships are. Everyone expects to get something in return for what they're giving. And if you misjudge the stakes or barter foolishly, offer what you cannot give, take what you do not want, the relationship won't last, or else, what is far worse, it will last for a long time, with each bitterly believing he was cheated, but too ashamed to admit it even to himself.

MARY. But you've not had his children have you?

POLLY. Of course not. A man expects his wife to bear his children and his mistress to bear none.

MARY. Yet you've won his affection.

POLLY. Yes, I have.

MARY. Why? How?

POLLY. By not even wanting it. I have always been honest with him. He knows all I want from him is a comfortable home. In exchange I've shown him a solicitous care. I've babied him, become his mother, his mistress. And I've always known the mistress was only incidental. I've let him become with me the little boy he wanted from you. When he was a boy his mother went insane. He saw in you that which had closed him off from her. The more outrageously you tried to gain his attention and sympathy, the more he turned away in loathing. Your behavior has made him come to hate you.

MARY. Has he said that to you?

POLLY. I can tell you his words exactly. "I hate her like the devil, and I note with pleasure that this feeling increases daily."

MARY. I don't believe you. He wouldn't say that. He wouldn't feel that.

POLLY. "I hate her like the devil, and I note with pleasure that this feeling increases daily."

MARY. I won't believe you. I can't.

POLLY. "I hate her like the devil, and I note with pleasure that this feeling increases daily."

MARY. What intolerable wrong did I do him?

POLLY. Perhaps he does not know himself. The fact is, however, you were not sensible. You see, it is never sensible to expect a man to understand or to tolerate the dreams of his wife. (POLLY *exits.*)

MARY. And they told him that I suffer from dreaming.

FURY #1. Oh. we got us some cures for dreamers here, Mary.

FURY #4. Dr. Rush gives special care to dreamers, Mary.

FURY #3. Some icy baths in winter.

FURY #5. Splinters under the thumbnails.

FURY #2. A white-hot iron on the soles of the feet for sanity.

MARY. But they would not do that to me, for they know I'm sane.

FURIES. How could they. Possibly. Know that?

MARY. They know it because it's true.

FURIES. Did they. Tell you. You are. Sane? Mary?

MARY. I know it. One can tell. Surely one can tell for oneself?

FURIES. No. They have to tell you. Tell you, Mary. Tell you.

MARY. Who can do that? The doctors? The Board of Managers?

FURIES. You can, Mary. It's easy as pie, Mary. Mary. Crazy Mary Girard. You can tell. If you really. Want. To. It's easy as pie Mary. Easy as making your bed. Gathering flowers. Listening. As simple as praying to God, Mary. God. God. Where are you God?

FURY #5. Do you ever pray, Mary?

MARY. What do you mean? Of course, I . . .

FURY #5. No, no, no, no. To really, really pray to Almighty God with all of your mind and all of your heart and all of your soul. To pray until His heart and His mind and His soul open out to you until you are riding there. Until you are riding there like crystal. Riding on beams of the purest, whitest, celestial crystal. O Jesus. My Saviour. Sweet, Sweet, Jesus . . .

FURIES. Jesus. Jesus. Sweet, Sweet Jesus.

MARY. And because of that you have . . .

FURY #1. Have ye never locked up a lock, Mary?

FURIES. Clickety clack. Clickety lock. Lock up the lock.

FURY #1. I have. Many times. Ye turns the key right in the lock big as a pie. Takes 'em with this hand, like this, an' puts 'em in, like this, an' turns the key in the lock, like this, big as a pie. Big as a pie. You turn the key right in the lock, big as a pie. Takes 'em with this hand like this, jus' like my daddy tole 'er, and puts 'em in, like this, an' turns the key in the lock, like this, big as a pie. Ye turns the key right in the . . .

FURIES. Lock big as a pie. Takes em with this hand. Clickety clack. Lock up the lock.

MARY. I don't understand what . . .

FURY #3. I would have understood. Exactly, Mary. Have you ever made your bed, Mary? It must be done, exactly. At the proper time. Not too late or improperly or too soon. Not just any way. The sheets must be smoothed and straightened well until no single line or wrinkle. Until no single line or wrinkle disturbs the weight of the counterpane that touches . . . And if the the covers are spread straight. Pillows fluffed up soft. Smoothest straight then. But if it is not as neat and as smooth as hair. It must be. It must not . . . It must be torn apart. One must begin . . . again. The sheets must have . . .

FURIES. No. Wrinkles. Mary. Smooth, Mary. As smooth as. Hair, Mary.

MARY. But how can you possibly. . . .

FURY #4. Have you listened, Mary. On the docks, I lifted . . . I lifted with the sweat . . . Hold. and Listen. Listen to the robin . . . Bales and . . . thrush. Heave for the nonce lad. Listen for the. Lift. Laugh. Laugh. No. Hold . . . Heave with the crank on. Hold. Falls all. No. Heave. Lips. Speak. Heave. No. Cry. Thunder. Asks. Why?. No. Hold. No. (*Scream*).

FURIES. Don't cry. Mary. You mustn't. Cry. Mary. Or listen. You mustn't scream, Mary.

FURY #2. You never gathered flowers, did you, Mary? I gathered more flowers than anyone has ever dreamed of. I had to hide them. Have you ever held a flower, Mary. Your very own flowers, Mary. Tender and secret and gentle. Hide it in your arms. You in your secret place. Did you rock with it, Mary. Rock until one by one the petals fall and the stem dries up and the cradle rocks. By yourself, Mary . . . Rock yourself, Mary.

FURIES. What can you tell, Mary. Tell us, Mary. Tell us about your. Self. Mary. Tell us. Tell. Us.

MARY. Afterward. The sounds of water lapping in the pail through the streets. And before. As I drew it from the well, for my arms were always strong.

FURIES. Yes. Mary? Mary? Yes. Yes?

MARY. The sounds of empty spaces in the water made by the dripping. By the sucking of the bucket. Brim-full. Lifting, lifting . . .

FURIES. Yes, Mary.

MARY. And . . . and sometimes as a little girl I stood beside my father to watch him working. The sound of his hammer hammering. Nails. . . .

FURIES. That's right, Mary. Yes.

MARY. The sound of the nails being driven and Him. . . . and him . . . Bring him to me.

FURIES. (*Afraid. Weeping. Trembling.*) We don't know. Who you. Mean. We daren't step. On any toes. We cannot . . .

MARY. (*Interrupting.*) Bring Stephen Girard. Bring him now into this cell.

FURIES. No, no. Oh no, we must. Not. We can. Not. No, no, no.

MARY. Bring him!

(GIRARD ENTERS. *He does not know where he is for a moment. The* FURIES *surround him and then hide behind him.*)

GIRARD. How did you get here?

MARY. I am where you placed me. Stephen.

GIRARD. Where I . . . I shouldn't be in this place.

MARY. (*Laughing.*) No, Stephen?

GIRARD. No, I . . .

MARY. (*Laughing.*) Do you think I'm a vision?

GIRARD. No. Of course not. I . . . no.

(MRS. HATCHER ENTERS *with* MR. PHILLIPS.)

MRS. HATCHER. Is it true as they say that the baby is that of Mary Girard's?

MR. PHILLIPS. The baby's origin is a matter of no importance, Mrs. Hatcher. You and Mr. Hatcher will receive the set sum for nursing the child just as you have with all the other children you have cared for in the past.

MRS. HATCHER. Yes, Mr. Phillips. I do appreciate you're calling on me again. My health is ever so much better now than it used to be.

MR. PHILLIPS. The past is past, Mrs. Hatcher.

MARY. Why have you done this to me?

GIRARD. I had no choice. You are insane.

MARY. Don't lie to me, Stephen. Even if I were insane you could have spared me this. Both you and I know what my behavior was. You know as well as I that I am sane.

GIRARD. I hope that is true.

MRS. HATCHER. Oh. Such a pretty little baby. And a girl. What is her name?

MARY. Her name is Mary!

MR. PHILLIPS. Call her whatever you wish. It is immaterial.

MRS. HATCHER. Oh, I shall take good care of this one, Mr. Phillips. There won't be no repeats of my old mistakes. I'm ever so much better now.

MR. PHILLIPS. I told you not to speak of the past, Mrs. Hatcher. Both for your sake and for the sake of the Hospital it is best if you keep hidden from your neighbors the source from which you've received this child.

MRS. HATCHER. (*Exiting.*) Oh, I shall love having her. I am truly grateful. I've never had a little girl before. I think I'll call you . . . Rose. Rose is my name, you see, and you will be my little girl.

MR. PHILLIPS. (*Calling after her.*) Mrs. Hatcher!

MARY. She told me you hated me like the devil. I didn't believe her until this moment.

GIRARD. Who told you that?

MR. PHILLIPS. (*Calling.*) Mrs. Hatcher!

MRS. HATCHER. (*Returning.*) Yes, Mr. Phillips?

MR. PHILLIPS. Mrs. Hatcher. I would caution you against becoming too fond of this child. It is, after all, a child born under unpropitious circumstances.

MRS. HATCHER. What do you mean, Mr. Phillips?

MR. PHILLIPS. I am asking you to treat it the same as you would any other child.

MRS. HATCHER. Oh, I will sir.

MR. PHILLIPS. Yes? Well, good. Yes, I would have you treat it just as though it were a . . . a normal child.

MRS. HATCHER. Isn't it a normal child, Mr. Phillips?

MR. PHILLIPS. Oh, I didn't mean to alarm you, Mrs. Hatcher. This baby seems normal, doesn't it? It needs all the care and attention other children require. Only there is a difference.

MRS. HATCHER. What difference, Mr. Phillips? Tell me, please.

MARY. Don't let him do this!

MR. PHILLIPS. It's mother is a patient among the insane.

MRS. HATCHER. Oh no!

MR. PHILLIPS. The baby has been born by and among those possessed of devils.

(*The* FURIES *dance.*)

MRS. HATCHER. God preserve us!

MR. PHILLIPS. Born by and among those possessed of devils.

MRS. HATCHER. God preserve us.

MR. PHILLIPS. By and among those possessed of devils.

MRS. HATCHER. God preserve us. (MRS. HATCHER *and* MR. PHILLIPS EXIT.)

MARY. Is that what I am to you? When we met I was sixteen, a servant carrying water through the streets. I laughed at everything then. And I was happy without even knowing it. Do you remember that girl, Stephen?

GIRARD. She does not exist, madam.

MARY. No. We destroyed her, you and I. Destroyed her utterly. Didn't you ever love her?

GIRARD. She was pretty. People noticed her. She was innocent, a trait few women have.

MARY. Innocent! And then she married you and she thought she had gained the whole world, and in reality gained only this little room.

GIRARD. She had everything she should have wanted.

MARY. The cost was too great.

GIRARD. It cost her nothing.

MARY. (*Laughing.*) Nothing! (*She laughs.*) What is the value of nothing, Mr. Girard? What is its price? Can you estimate the enormity of nothing? I can tell you it is beyond calculation. I was prepared to give you everything, but you wanted only nothing. So it is fitting that you have placed me here in this room with nothing.

GIRARD. You had everything a woman could reasonably have wanted.

MARY. What good is reason without some little affection?

GIRARD. If you wanted affection you should have told me instead of making a public display of yourself.

MARY. Stephen, I made no attempt to hide my behavior from you. We differed in only one way. I didn't bring my lovers under your roof. You cannot fault me for that. I always maintained a respect for you and a regard for your feelings and your pride. Perhaps I should not have done the things I did. But in that I am not alone. Don't lock me up in this poor house. Send me away, Stephen. I will go wherever you wish. Take me back to one of your houses and lock me in a room for the rest of my life. Give me my father's tools, nails and a hammer, and I will drive the demons away from me. Lock me in a room; allow me there to suffer my conscience and dream my dreams alone.

GIRARD. Alone! A seclusive wife pleases no one. The needs of my sex are fewer than those of yours, madam. Men are more self-sufficient. Consequently, it is all the more important for a man's wife to see to it that his needs are met. Your acknowledgement of me as your husband never went beyond the duties of the flesh.

MARY. You mean to say my thoughts were my own?

GIRARD. I mean to say you failed to be a dutiful wife. When I found you you were a peasant. Your mother remains one. I had hoped you would develop a sense of who you had become in becoming my wife. I had hoped you would rise above your origins sufficiently to modify an overly tolerant nature. It is well-known that the wife of Stephen Girard converses indiscriminately with persons of no consequence as readily as she does with persons of some social standing. In these ways, and others, you have failed me.

(*Pause.*)

MARY. Yes, you are right. In these ways I have failed you, Stephen. (MARY *turns from him and starts to exit.*)

GIRARD. If only you could . . .

MARY. No!

GIRARD. I can make your life a hell on earth, madam.

MARY. When I was childless you blamed me. I too thought I was barren. I felt I had cheated you out of a son. But it wasn't me. You couldn't put life in my body because you had none in your own. I got more warmth from a stranger in a little hour than you could ever give. It isn't my child that is loathsome to you, Mr. Girard, but the freedom of my mind and my love of life itself. May God have pity on you, sir.

GIRARD. God? (*Pause. Very calmly.*) I do not know if God exists. If I thought he did I would pray that he keep you here for ever so long a time. As I cannot be sure of him, I will see to it myself that you endure a hell on earth. And I will pray to a possible God that it may endure forever. (GIRARD EXITS.)

MARY. All right. All right. But my baby will live.

FURIES. She thinks her baby . . . She thinks her infant . . . She thinks her child . . . Will give her comfort. Will give her solace. Will bring her relief. Not so, Mary. Oh no, no. No. You were untrue, Mary. You cuckolded your husband. You betrayed him. And broke your marriage vows. For shame. Shame, Mary. You will give birth to an evil thing. Only evil comes from evil. Something dark and horrid comes from evil. Darkness bred in darkness gives forth darkness. As we have shown you the head. As we have shown you the heart. As we have shown you the past. As we have shown you what the far future holds. So we will now show you what is yet to be. (FURIES *place the bundle in* MARY's *arms.*)

MARY. She is so . . . so very lovely. If I ever doubted that you were worth so much suffering forgive me. (*To* FURIES *who are in glee.*) Why are you looking like . . . laughing . . . laughing? Tell me. Tell me. She will live, won't she?

FURIES. Oh yes. Doubtlessly. Most definitely.

MARY. And she will be happy? Tell me. Will she be happy?

FURIES. Most certainly. Decidedly. Assuredly. Quite as happy as she could be. Most decidedly happy.

MARY. Then I shall live for that if you will promise me that.

FURIES. Oh, yes. We can do that. Yes. The question. However. Is. How long?

MARY. How long?

FURIES. It will not be. A longish. Life.

MARY. Will she die young?

FURIES. (*Taking the bundle from her.*) She will. Yes. Quite. Quite young.

MARY. Quite young? Will she live twenty years?

FURIES. Twenty! Heavens! What an age!

MARY. Fifteen years?

FURIES. Goodness no! Certainly. Not!

MARY. Then ten years, surely ten?

FURIES. Gracious goodness no. Nothing like it. Far from it.

MARY. Then five? A little five?

FURIES. Yes, Mary. Yes, indeed. You've hit on it.

MARY. My poor dear little child. Only five brief years of life.

FURIES. Oh, wrong! Years? We said nothing. About. Years.

MARY. But you just now said five. . . .

FURIES. Months. Mary. Yes. Months. Five. Five months. Yes. Yes.

MARY. No! Oh no! My little one.

FURIES. Five months. Is. Quite enough. Then buried. In an unmarked grave. That you will have in common. Mary. You too will be buried in an unmarked grave. Here. On the hospital grounds. You'll never leave these walls. Mary. And no services. Oh no, Mary. No hymns nor prayers for you. A burial. No services.

MARY. Good! That at least I delight to hear. And tell me when. The sooner the better will best suit me. If God has any mercy it will be soon. Tell me.

FURIES. Guess! We couldn't just say. Oh no, you'll have to guess.

MARY. A year?

FURIES. So short a time? Heavens. No.

MARY. Two? Three? Five? Surely no more than five.

FURIES. Yes, five! Five is right again! So clever is our Mary. Five. And twenty. Twenty. Twenty. More.

MARY. Twenty more? Five and twenty years? I could not stand it.

FURIES. Well, most of it. Will be. There. In this chair. The tranquilizing chair. The restraining chair. Bound down. Like the evil. Thing you are.

MARY. No! No! God would not permit it. He would not keep me living here in this hell hole for five and twenty years. I couldn't bear it. He will be merciful to me and let me die soon. Soon! Please dear God, sweet, sweet Jesus, be merciful to me and let me not stay here for such an age.

FURIES. Oh, isn't she funny! Sweet, sweet Jesus! Jesus! She's starting to frothe at the mouth in prayer. God won't hear you either, Mary. No more than Mr. Phillips. Why should He? He's too busy. Besides He's set you up for it. It's God's jest, Mary. And the fool is. You!

MARY. Get away from me. I won't listen to you. Please God, please!

FURIES. He made you beautiful. God did. And you made the mistake of believing in your own beauty. It's played you a devilish trick. It's been your doing. And your undoing. It's played you a devil of a trick. God did it to you. Too. Mary.

MARY. God, help me. Help me!

FURIES. Look at her. Oh, I love it when she prays to dark corners and damp walls. To empty spaces between the stars. If she could see any stars. Can you, Mary? Can you. See. Any stars?

MARY. I don't know. My eyesight is so dim.

Furies. It always happens. After long confinement. In dark places.

Mary. Where are you God? Please answer me.

Furies. Please answer me! Oh. Where. Are. You. God. God. God.

Mary. Stop it. Damn you. All of you. Where is He? And who is He? Is He another man? Then I'll have nothing to do with such a God. And I damn you, God. I damn you!

Furies. Do you hear? She's now giving proof. That she's. insane. Insane. Insane folks always deny God. They have to. They're the Devil's own. His handiwork. His cohorts. His consorts. Maybe she's the Devil's bitch. The Devil's whore. Maybe she's sucked bile from the Devil's own tit. And filled her belly with his swollen prick. Mary, the Devil's trick. Mary Girard, the Devil's harlot, the Devil's cat, the Devil's bat, the Devil's meretrix! When they discover how she's cursed God . . .

Mary. Leave me alone!

Furies. And turned on Him . . .

Mary. Don't touch me.

Furies. And denounced and damned Him . . . .

Mary. Stop!

Furies. Then maybe they'll tear the babe from her bleeding belly. Condemn it for a cursed thing. Pull it with pinchers from her Devil's doorway. Kick it. Tromp on it. Spit on it. Damn it. Curse it. Pull it. Tear it. Bury it living. Burn it with firesticks. Break it with stones.

Mary. STOP!

Furies. Now she's caught our scent. Like hounds behind the fox. Let's hope. She's quick. To. Make the. Leap. At last. She. Understands!

Mary. Yes. At last I do understand. (*Pause.*) What

if I were insane and didn't even know? I think I wouldn't care. The bed is firm. There is a window there that I could look from if I stood atop the bed. If I were calm they would not always keep me in this chair. If I were to accept you as my companions and not resist you. . . . I could walk about. Take some few steps. Look from the window. Sometimes I might see the sky. Smell the air. Give birth to my poor, pitiful child. Isn't that true?

FURIES. (*Softly.*) Yes. Mary. Yes. Yes. Indeed.

MARY. And if I were to turn my back on that world, and scorn all the values it adores, denying myself the luxury wealth can provide, then that must stand as proof that I am insane, wouldn't it?

FURIES. Yes! Oh, yes! Yes. Yes.

MARY. For here is only poverty, solitude, and deprivation, where there, in the great world, is wealth, endless self-indulgence, and the society of ordinary people such as him, Mr. Stephen Girard. And if I were to prefer all this to all that, then the world would know me to be mad, wouldn't they?

FURIES. Yes, certainly. Most assuredly, Mary. Definitely so, Mary.

MARY. Then if I am not mad already, I soon shall be. For there is a point in my mind, a point of absolute stillness where hatred, jealously, and greed cannot come. A point of feeling, of being which longing and unhappiness cannot touch. And when I pull myself into that place I feel as though I'd reached something like God, but greater, far greater than God. And going there I can look out on my little life as though it were a shadow show upon a wall. And all is quiet and gentle and peaceful there for no human being can enter. And by comparison the world outside is horrid with greed, and heartless and cruel. So let them come to the windows to point and laugh at me. I will show them the respect they warrant. Dare let them come. I shall give them the show they expect and deserve. I will greet them with venom, caress them with violence and address them with words obscene and gestures which are vulgar. I shall look them boldly in the eyes to curse them and spit on them from the depths of a well of hatred, for I shall teach them that they are nothing more than a fart in the face of God. And tear off my clothes to show them my netherparts so they can plainly see how completely I repudiate their world in order to enter this. And I shall have nothing to lose. And it shall be no capitulation or surrender. For, from this day, I, Mary Girard, shall be truly and happily insane. Insane. Insane. Insane. Insane. Insane. Insa . . .

(*During the latter half of the above speech, the* FURIES *have very cautiously placed* MARY *in the restrain-in chair. On the line, "And I shall have nothing to lose" the* BELLS *of the churches peel throughout the city. In the midst of* MARY'S *final word, one of the more daring of the* FURIES *drops the box down over* MARY'S *head, so the sound of the word is cut-off.* FURIES EXIT. LIGHTS *stay up on* MARY *in the restraining chair, then they slowly begin to fade and suddenly* BLACKOUT. *Bells continue chiming and grow in volume, then stop.*)

END

PROPERTY LIST

Tranquilizing chair (A chair with leather straps to bind the arms and legs of the person sitting in it. It also has a square wooden box that fits over the head.)
Keys, broom, pail and ladle for Warder
A cape, hat and muff for Mary
Wooden bowls and cups for each inmate
Shawl and flowers for Mrs. Lum
Desk, two chairs, quill pen and papers for Mr. Girard
Baby-shaped bundle for Mary, then for Mrs. Hatcher.

PRODUCTION NOTES

Whether done on a proscenium stage or in the round each inmate of the asylum should be assigned his/her own space on-stage as his/her own cell. These areas should be the places to which each returns when not enacting one of Mary's memories or fantasies. The tranquilizing chair should be most prominently located at all times. Above it if possible, should be a platform on which is Mr. Girard's room for the Mr. Philips-Mr. Girard scene. Thus, if Mary is in the chair the scene is being enacted directly above her. Vocally the most important element is the division of text among the furies. The more extensive the breakdown of the text among them the more startling is the effect. They should be placed on stage far enough away from one another so that the sound will surround Mary (and the audience as well if possible.)

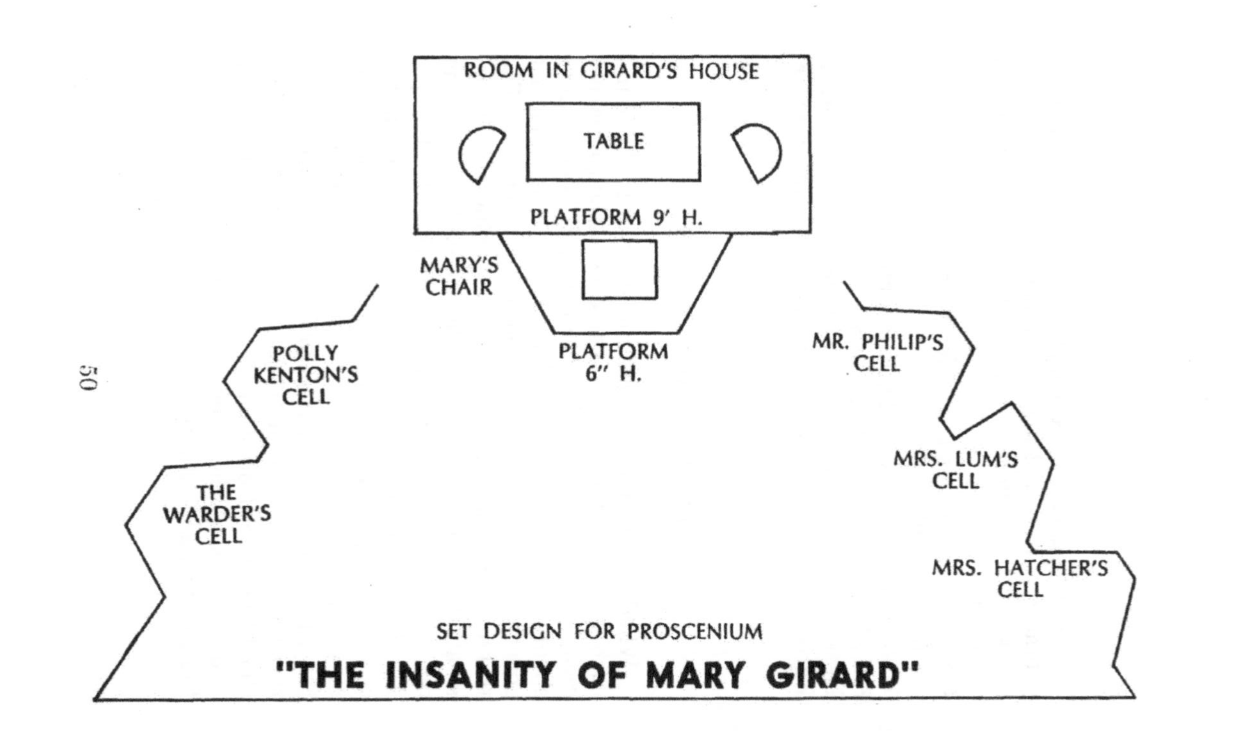
ROOM IN GIRARD'S HOUSE
TABLE
PLATFORM 9' H.
MARY'S CHAIR
PLATFORM 6" H.
POLLY KENTON'S CELL
THE WARDER'S CELL
MR. PHILIP'S CELL
MRS. LUM'S CELL
MRS. HATCHER'S CELL
SET DESIGN FOR PROSCENIUM
"THE INSANITY OF MARY GIRARD"

Also By

Lanie Robertson

BACK COUNTY CRIMES

LADY DAY AT EMERSON'S BAR AND GRILL

NASTY LITTLE SECRETS

OTHER TITLES AVAILABLE FROM SAMUEL FRENCH

THE RIVERS AND RAVINES
Heather McDonald

Drama / 9m, 5f / Unit Set

Originally produced to acclaim by Washington D.C.'s famed Arena Stage. This is an engrossing political drama about the contemporary farm crisis in America and its effect on rural communities.

"A haunting and emotionally draining play. A community of farmers and ranchers in a small Colorado town disintegrates under the weight of failure and thwarted ambitions. Most of the farmers, their spouses, children, clergyman, banker and greasy spoon proprietress survive, but it is survival without triumph. This is an *Our Town* for the 80's."
– *The Washington Post*

SAMUELFRENCH.COM